HOW TO D™

IN 3D

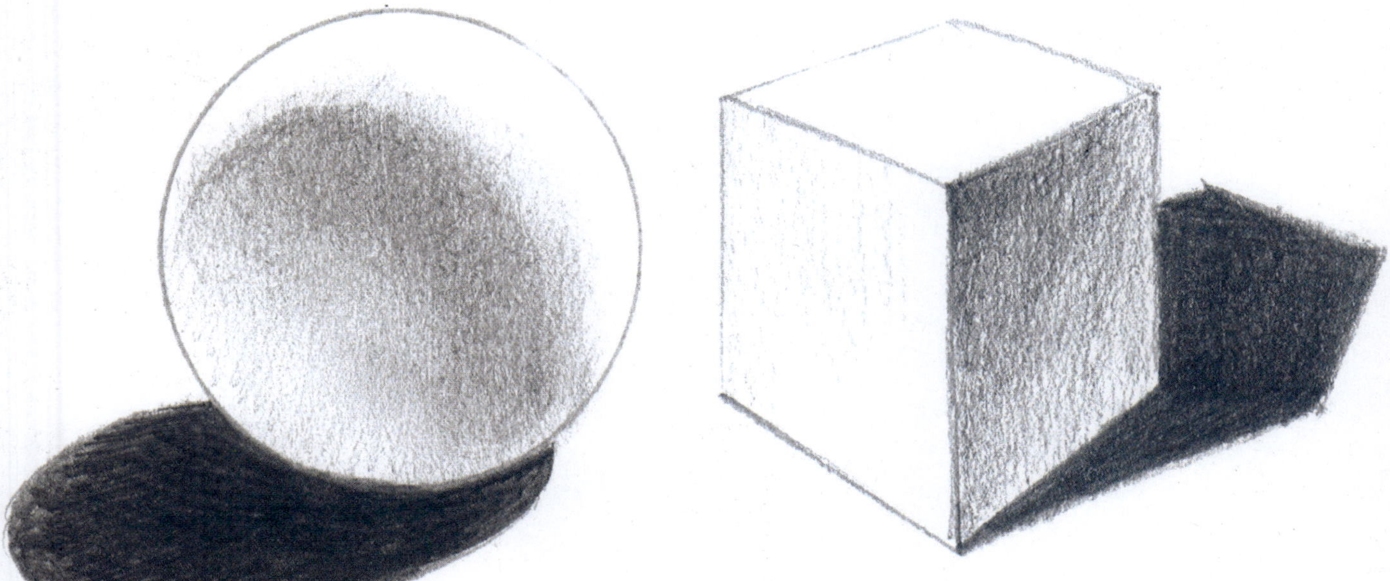

Mark Bergin

BOOK HOUSE

SALARIYA

Published in Great Britain in MMXVI by
Book House, an imprint of
The Salariya Book Company Ltd
25 Marlborough Place, Brighton BN1 1UB

1 3 5 7 9 8 6 4 2

Author: Mark Bergin was born in Hastings in 1961. He studied at Eastbourne College of Art and has specialised in historical reconstructions as well as aviation and maritime subjects since 1983. He lives in Bexhill-on-Sea with his wife and three children.

Editor: Nick Pierce

PB ISBN: 978-1-910706-54-1

A CIP catalogue record for this book is available from the British Library.

Printed and bound in China.
Printed on paper from sustainable sources.

WARNING: Fixatives should be used only under adult supervision.

Contents

Perspective

Perspective is a way of drawing things so that they appear to be in three dimensions. When you look at an object in real life, the parts of it that are close to your eye look larger than the parts that are further away. Things that are really the same width, such as railway lines, appear to get narrower as they vanish into the distance. If you copy this effect in your drawing, you can trick the eye into seeing in 3D.

These trees are all the same height, but the further ones look smaller and closer together than the nearer ones. The two rows of trees are parallel, but perspective makes them appear to meet in the far distance. This is an example of simple one-point perspective (see pages 6–7).

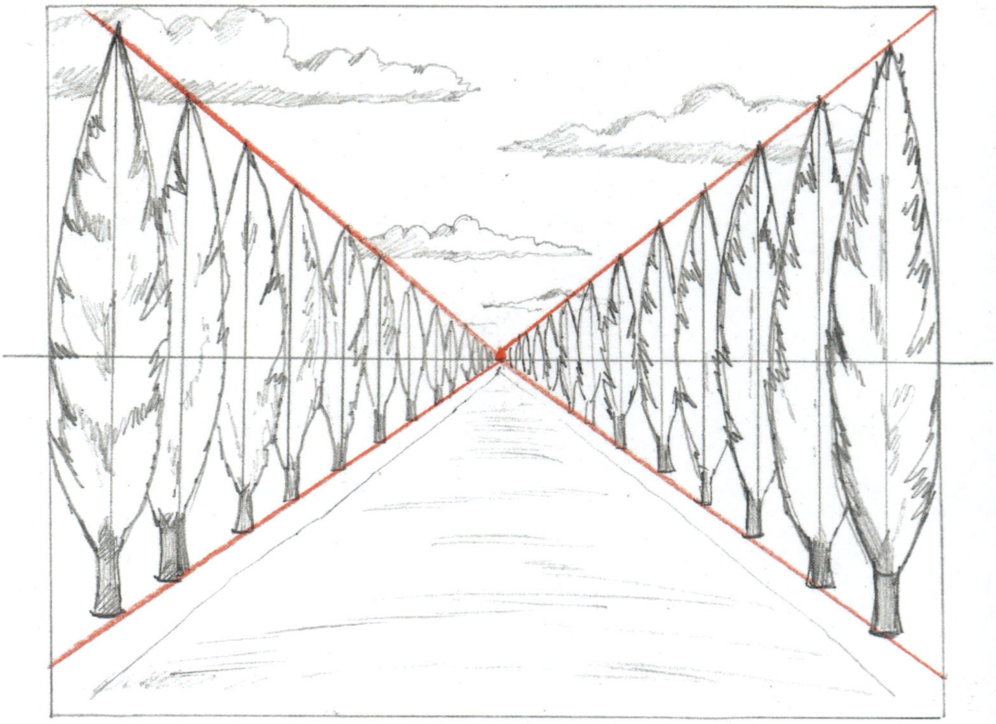

Imagine you are looking through a window at an object in the distance. Rays of light from the object pass through the window and reach your eyes. If you could trace exactly what you see on the glass, you would have a picture in perfect perspective.

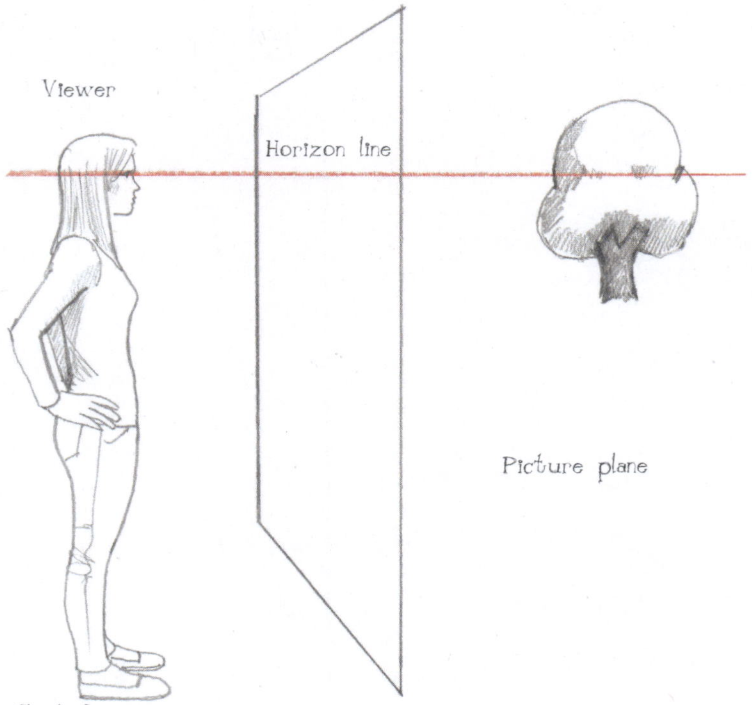

The **horizon** is the line in the far distance where earth and sky seem to meet. It is always level with the viewer's eye. The **picture plane** is that imaginary window between the viewer and the object viewed.

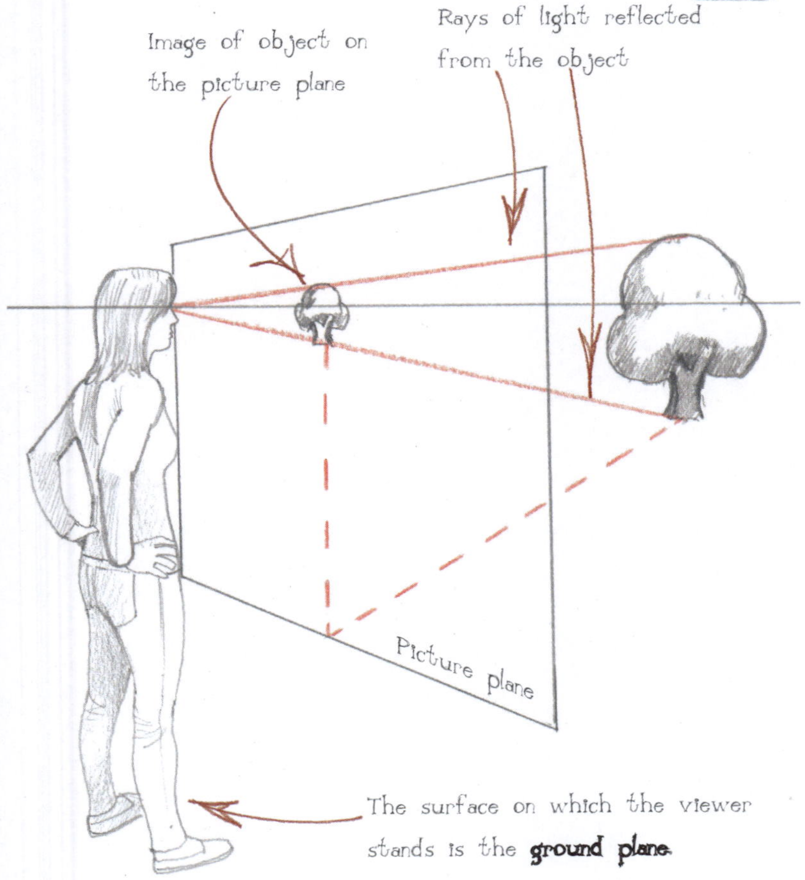

You see the object through the rays of light that are reflected off it. The image you want to draw is formed where these rays of light meet the picture plane. The distance between the viewer, the picture plane and the object determines how big the object will appear in the final drawing.

Vanishing points

The place in the far distance where parallel lines appear to meet is the **vanishing point.** In simple one-point perspective there is only one vanishing point, and it is on the horizon.

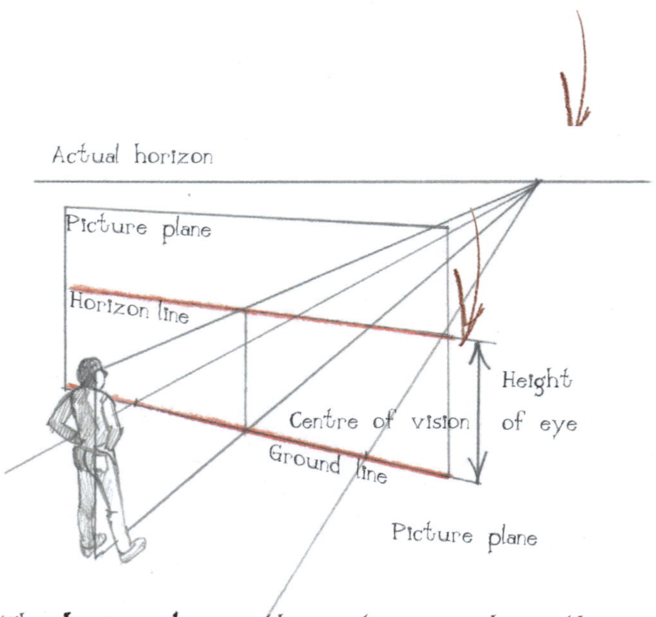

The **horizon line** in the picture is where the light rays reflected from the actual horizon meet the picture plane. The horizon is always level with the viewer's **eye level** (the height of the viewer's eye above the ground plane). The **centre of vision** is the point on the horizon exactly opposite the viewer's eye. The **ground line** is where the picture plane meets the ground plane.

One-point perspective

In one-point perspective, lines that lead away from the viewer (such as the sides of the road in this picture) meet at the vanishing point on the horizon. Vertical or horizontal lines that are parallel to the viewer (such as the walls of the buildings facing us) remain vertical or horizontal in the picture as well.

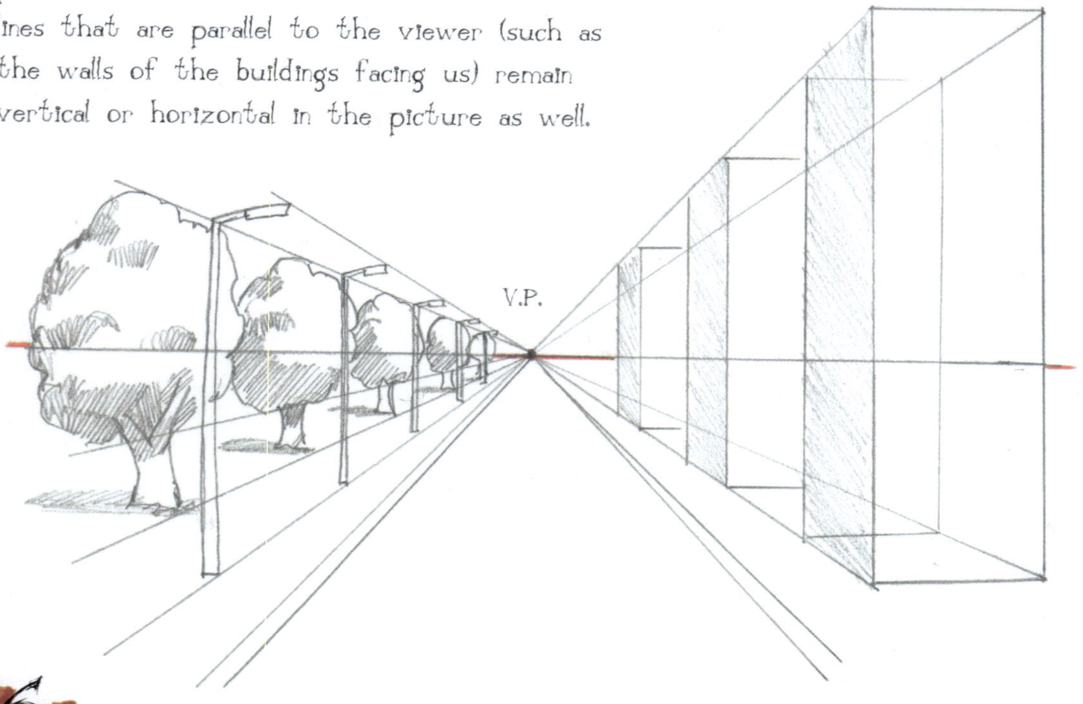

V.P. = vanishing point

One-point perspective is used when one side of the object is parallel to the viewer, such as when you are looking at a building head-on. If the object is at an angle to the viewer, such as when you are standing to one side of a building and looking at the corner of it, you need to use two-point perspective.

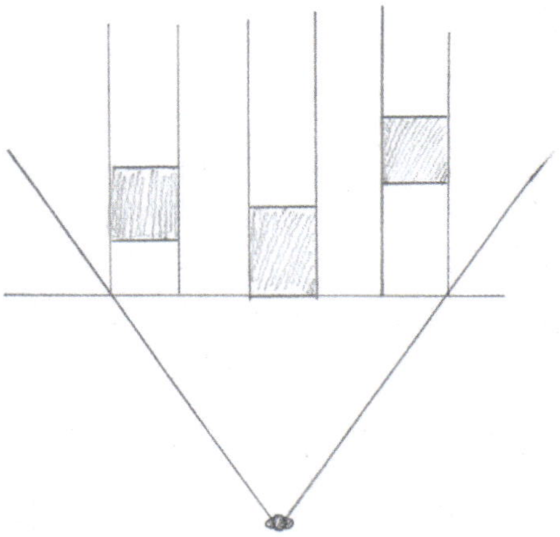

In this plan view we see a person looking at three buildings. One side of each building faces the viewer.

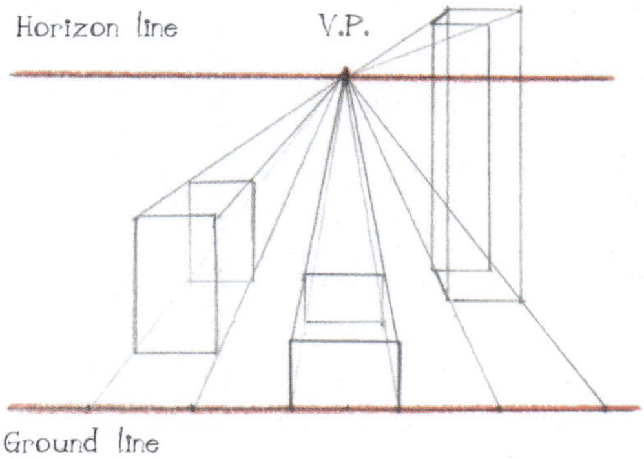

This is how the viewer sees the three buildings, in one-point perspective.

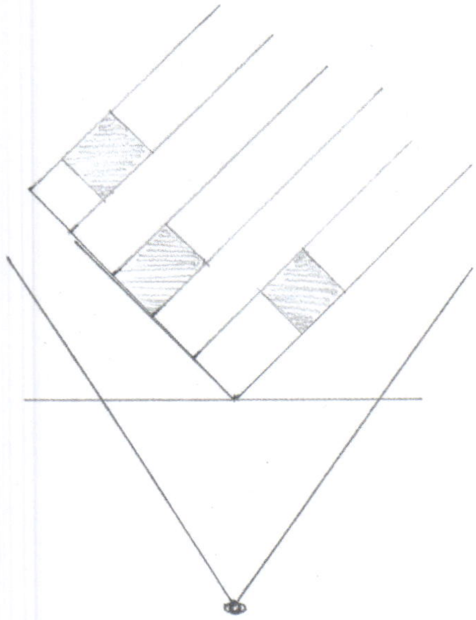

In this plan view, the person is looking from the corner and can see two sides of each building.

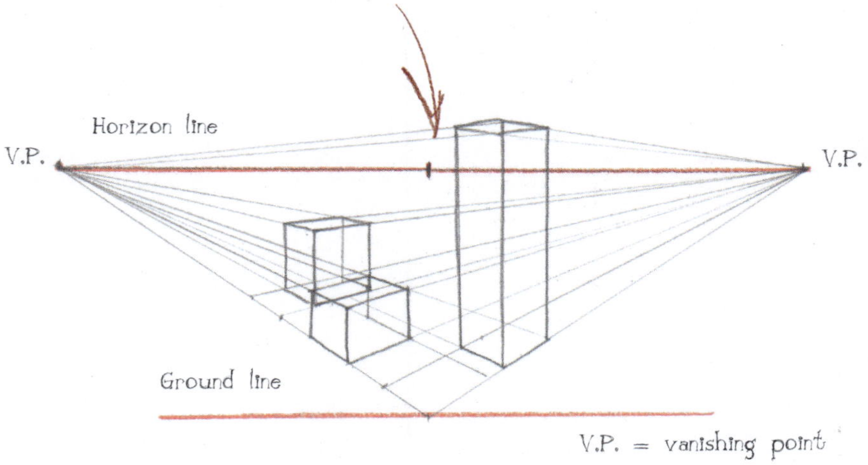

This is how the three buildings appear to the viewer in two-point perspective.

Changing viewpoints

These examples all show the same cube drawn from different positions.

In the examples on this page, the front face of the cube is parallel to the viewer. The viewer sees the cube in one-point perspective.

1. Cube straight ahead of the viewer, at the centre of vision.

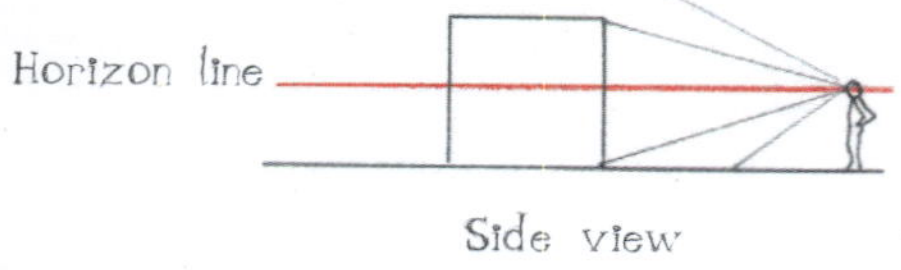

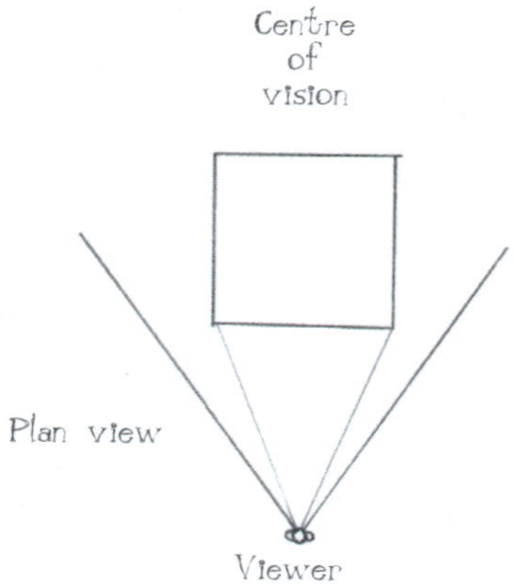

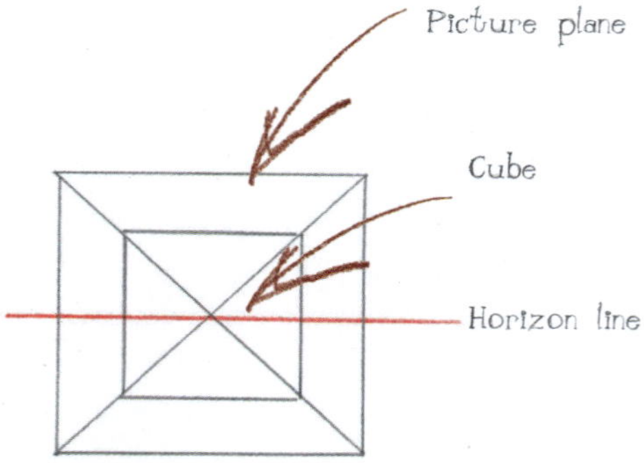

The viewer sees only the front face of the cube.

2. Cube to the left of the viewer. Viewer is looking straight ahead.

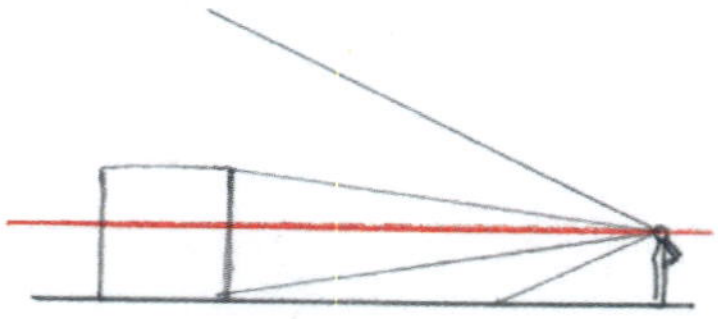

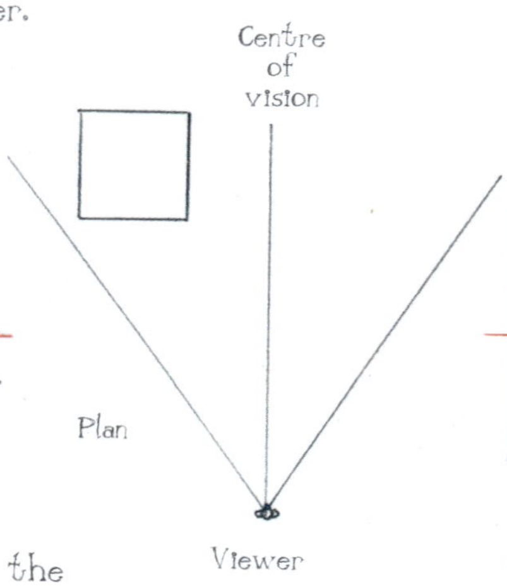

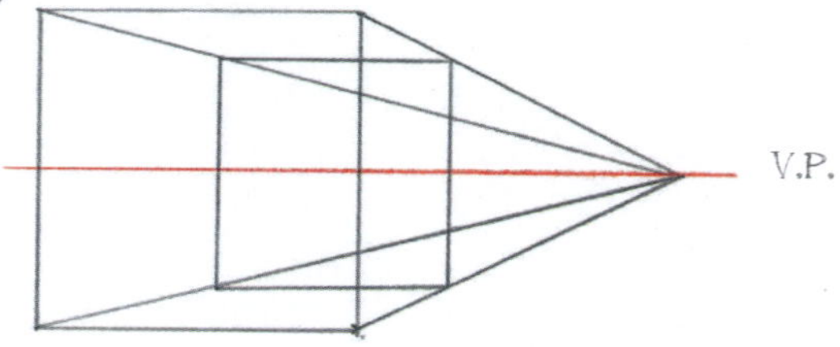

The viewer sees the front and right sides of the cube in one-point perspective.

3. Cube below the viewer and to the right. Viewer is looking straight ahead.

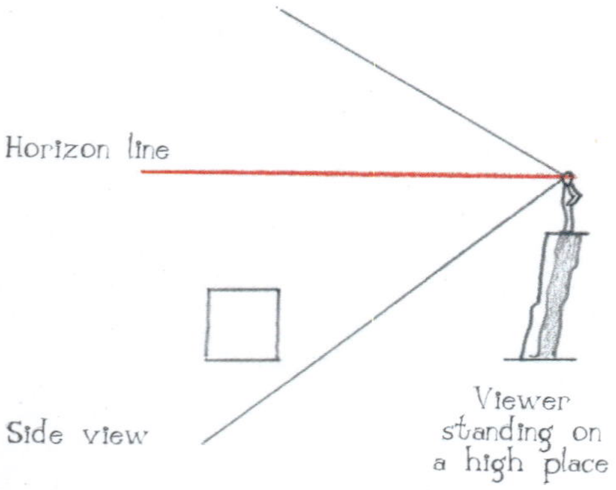

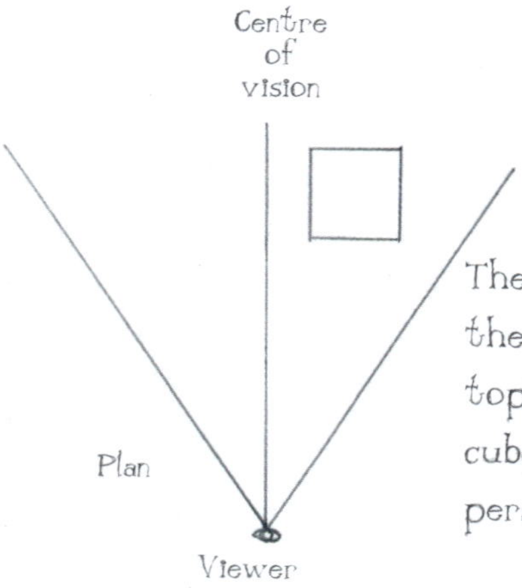

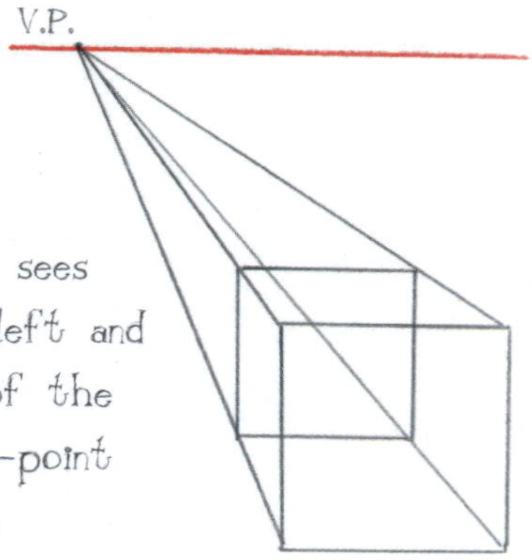

The viewer sees the front, left and top faces of the cube in one-point perspective.

Two-point perspective

In the examples on this page, the cube is turned so that the viewer can see two sides at once. Each side converges towards its own separate vanishing point on the horizon. This is called two-point perspective. In two-point perspective, lines which are vertical on the real object are vertical in the drawing also.

1. The cube is directly opposite the viewer, with two sides facing the viewer.

Side view

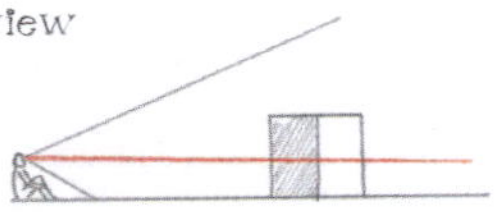

Plan

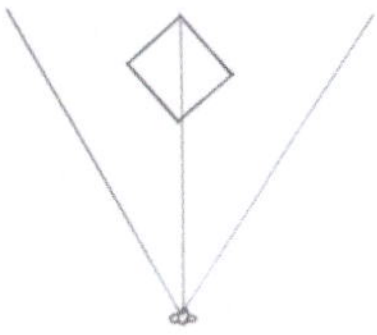

Viewer

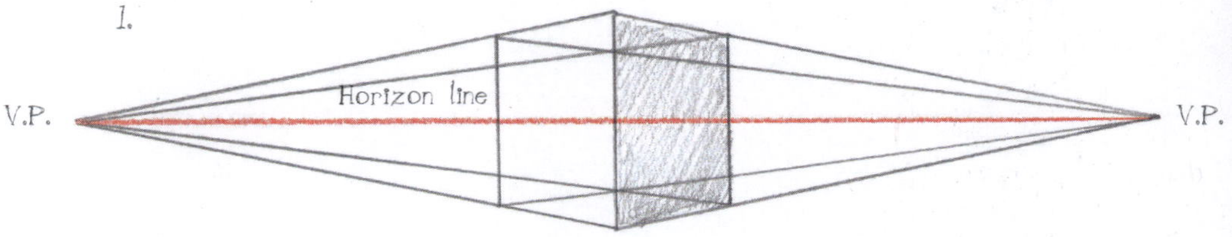

The viewer sees two sides of the cube in two-point perspective. Because the cube is at the centre of vision, the viewer sees equal amounts of both sides.

2. The cube is directly opposite the viewer, and below the viewer's eye level.

Side view

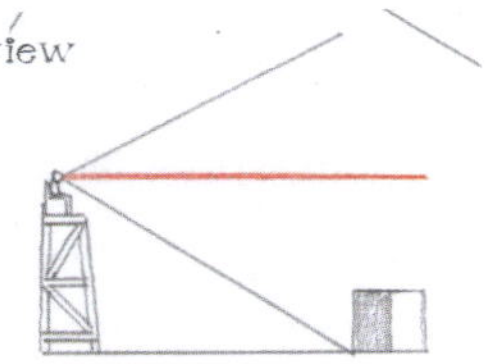

Plan

Viewer standing on a high place

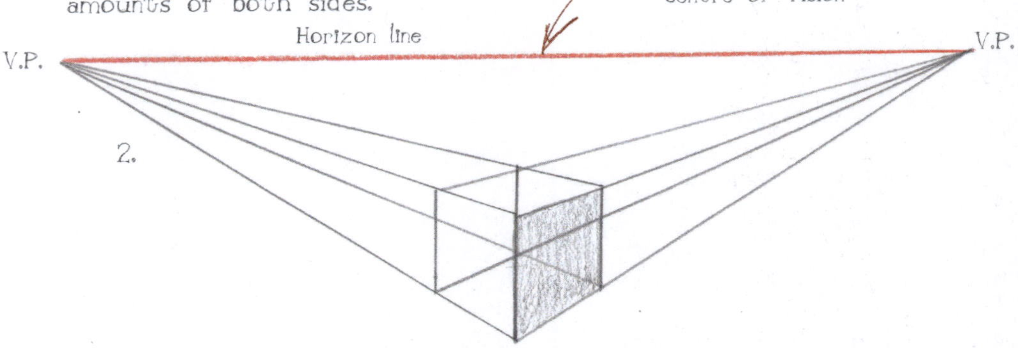

The viewer sees two sides and the top of the cube in two-point perspective. Again the viewer sees equal amounts of both sides of the cube.

3. The cube is to the right of the viewer, and above the viewer's eye level.

Side view

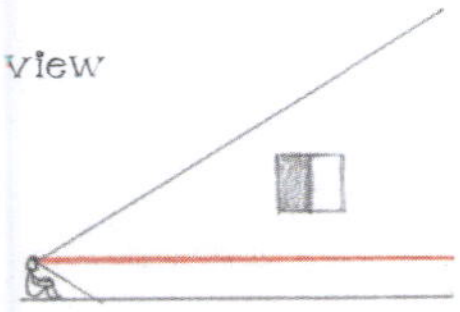

Plan

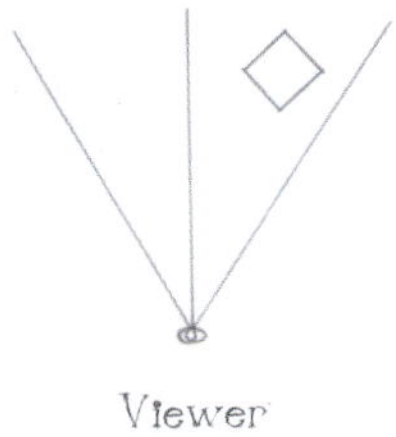

Viewer

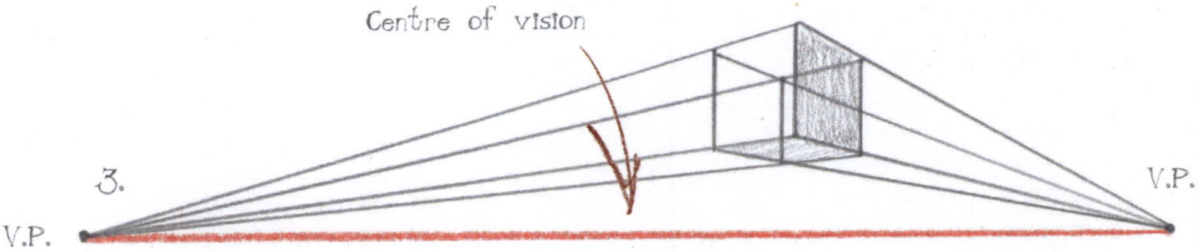

The viewer sees two sides and the underside of the cube in two-point perspective. Because the cube is to the right of the centre of vision, the viewer sees more of the left side of the cube than the right side.

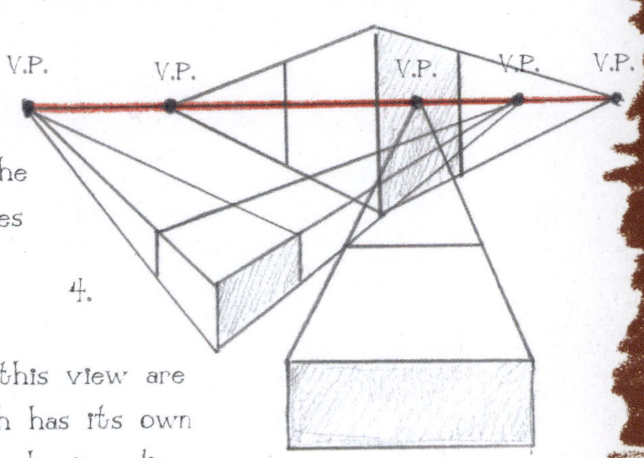

4. Because the three cubes in this view are not parallel to one another, each has its own separate vanishing points on the horizon line.

Looking up or down

Three-point perspective is used when the viewpoint is either very low or very high. Aerial or ground-level photos of skyscrapers create dramatic viewpoints that are a good way of showing how three-point perspective works.

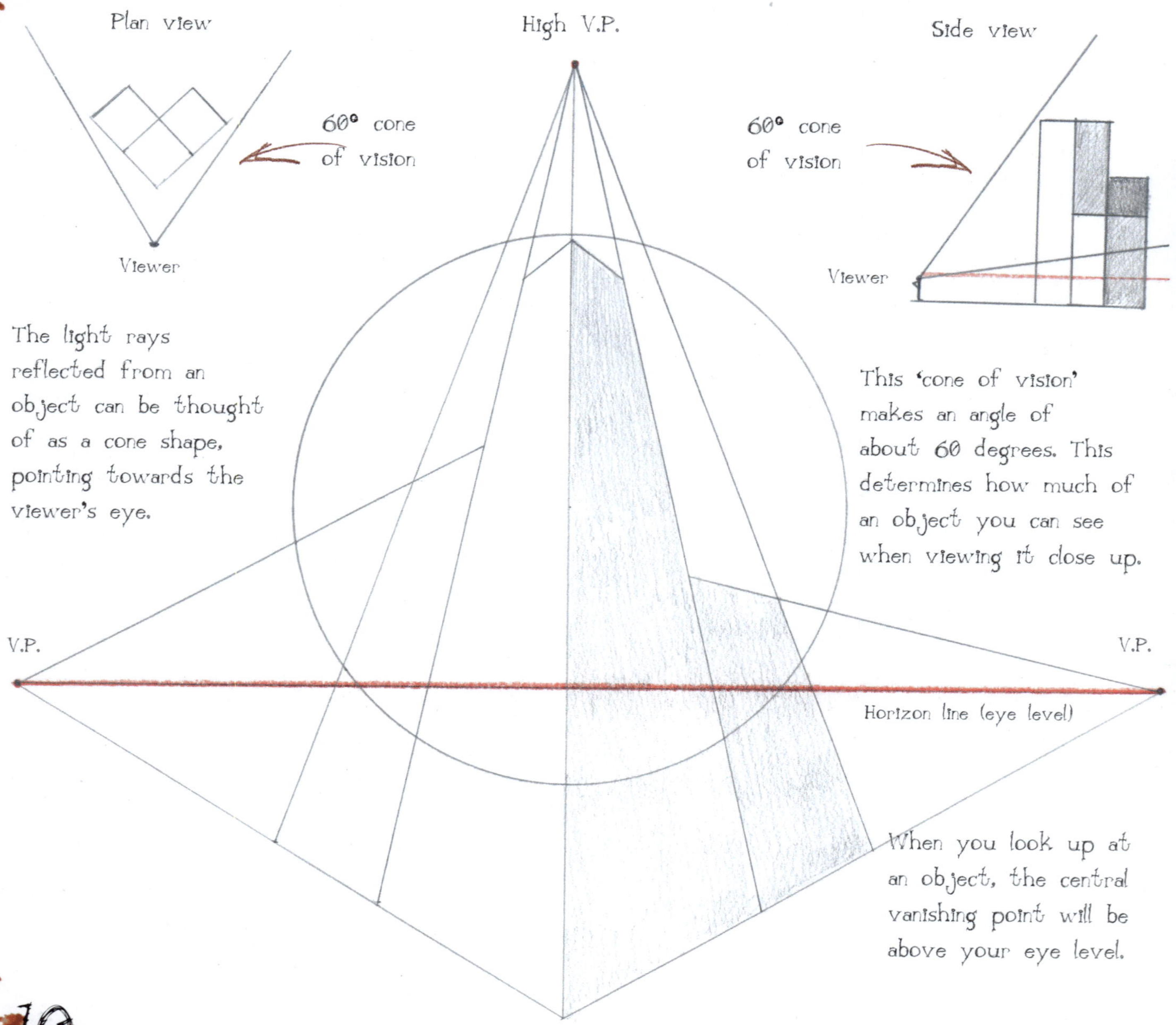

The light rays reflected from an object can be thought of as a cone shape, pointing towards the viewer's eye.

This 'cone of vision' makes an angle of about 60 degrees. This determines how much of an object you can see when viewing it close up.

When you look up at an object, the central vanishing point will be above your eye level.

A high-level view means that the sides of the buildings dramatically converge towards a low vanishing point. The tops of the buildings will also be visible.

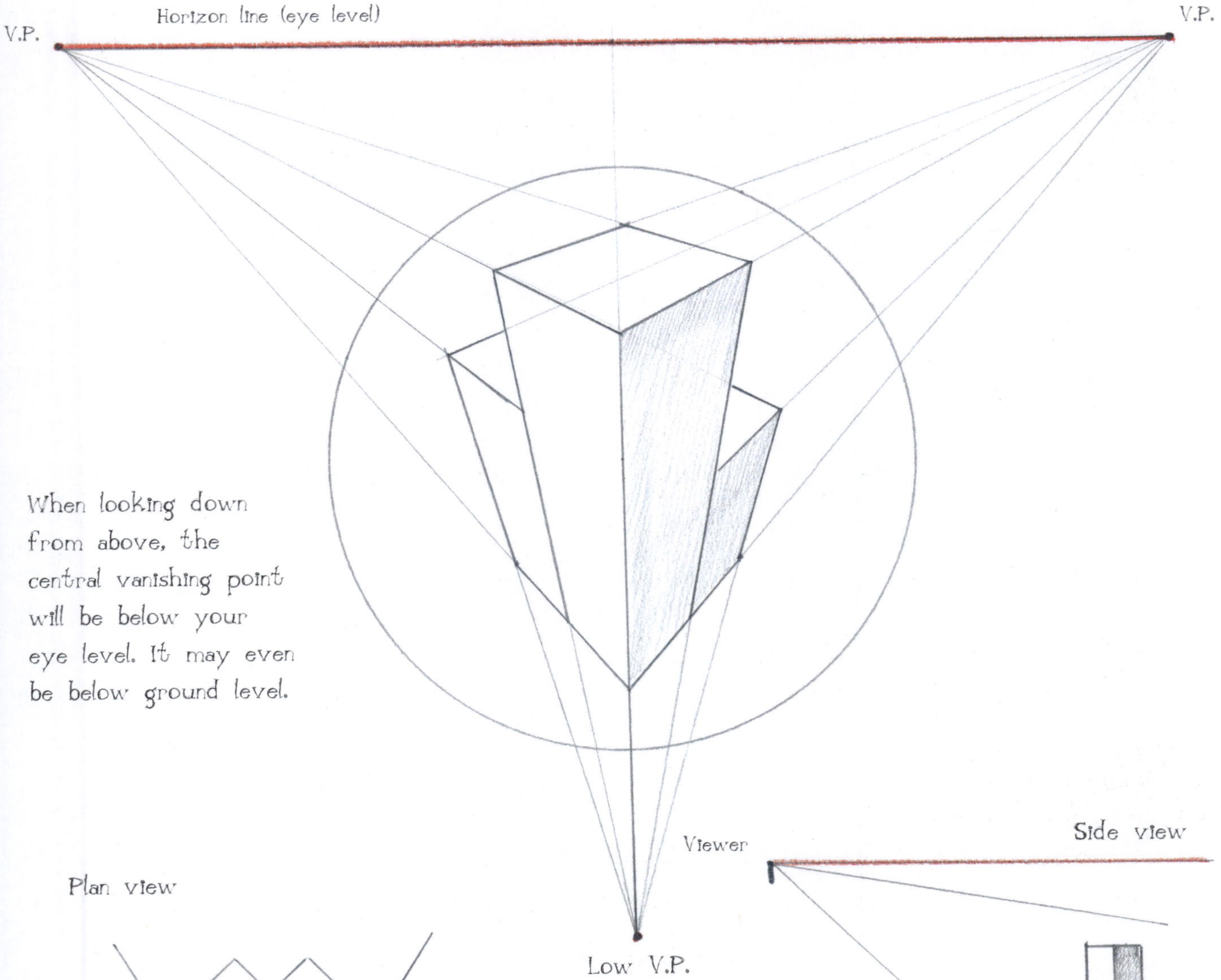

When looking down from above, the central vanishing point will be below your eye level. It may even be below ground level.

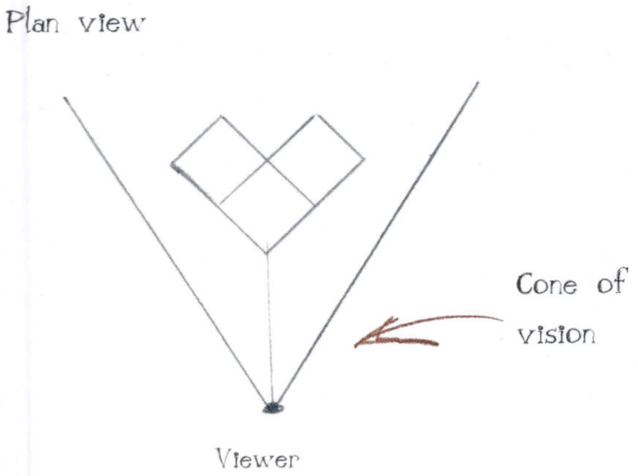

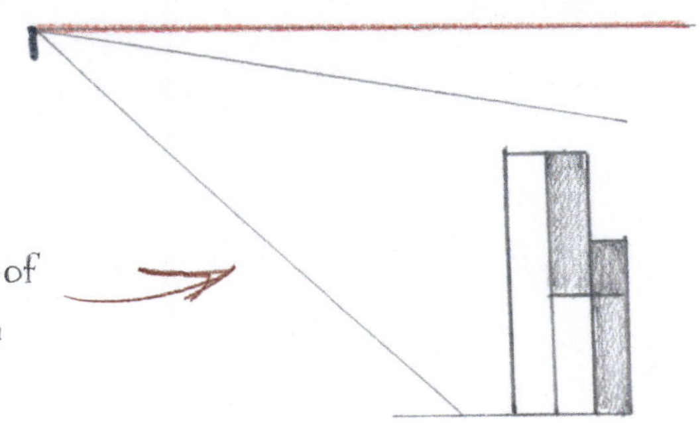

In three-point perspective, lines which are vertical or horizontal in real life (such as the walls of these skyscrapers) are always shown sloping in the drawing, unless they are exactly in line with the centre of vision.

Defining form

The way light hits an object helps define its form. Using light and shade can make an object appear three-dimensional.

In this view the light comes from behind and the sphere casts an almost circular shadow. The areas of shading on the sphere are furthest from the light source, facing the viewer.

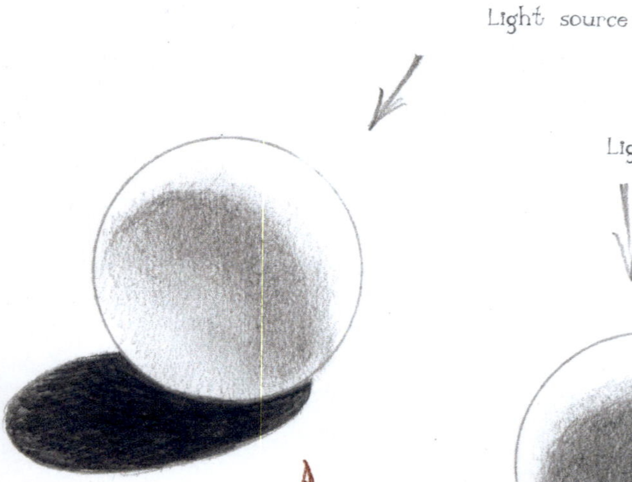

In this view the light comes from the side and the sphere casts an elliptical shadow.

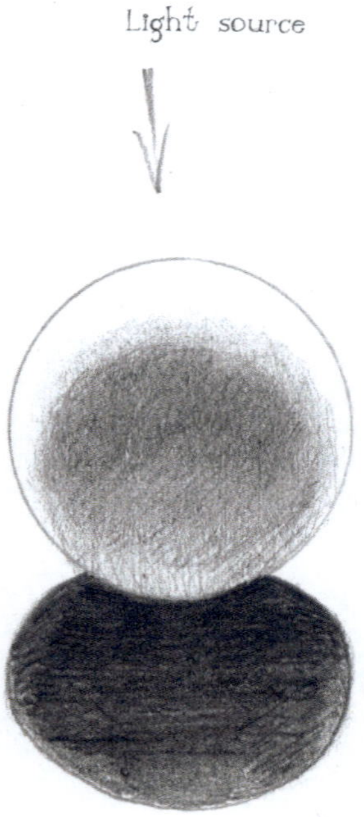

In this view the light comes from above the sphere and casts an elliptical shadow. Note how this light source creates a much lower area of shading on the sphere.

Here are some samples of light sources helping to define the shape of different objects.

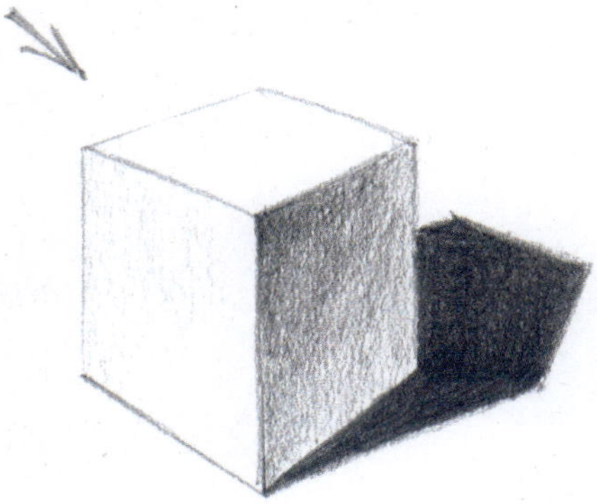

These shading techniques can then be used to define the shapes in your still life. Using different levels of shade will affect the overall tone of your drawing.

Light and shade

Light and shade play a major role in the outcome of your drawing. It is well worth considering the direction and strength of your light source. Both aspects add an important dimension to 3D drawing.

This drawing is front-lit with a strong light source. The object itself has little shading but it casts a strong shadow on the wall behind it.

In this still-life arrangement, the soft lighting comes from the right-hand side. Therefore the shading is mostly on the left side of the objects. Because they are brightly lit, the shading is quite muted. Cross-hatching is a good shading technique.

The light source in this still life comes from quite a low angle and casts dark shadows. The objects are heavily shaded because of the low lighting.

Artificial light can create interesting light and shade effects. The light source in this still life comes from the lamp at the centre of the composition. The light hits all the objects at different angles, so shadows are cast in different directions. The lampshade also glows because the light source is inside it.

Composition

Try framing your drawing with a square or a rectangle – this can make it look completely different.

Yellow NY taxi

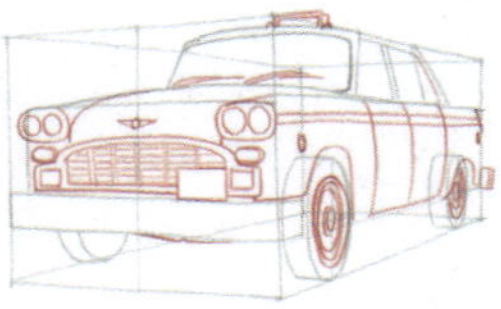

The act of flagging down a taxi cab is called 'hailing'; just stick your arm out above your head, and pretend you're the Statue of Liberty.

When drawing complex objects it is easiest to begin by drawing a box in perspective.

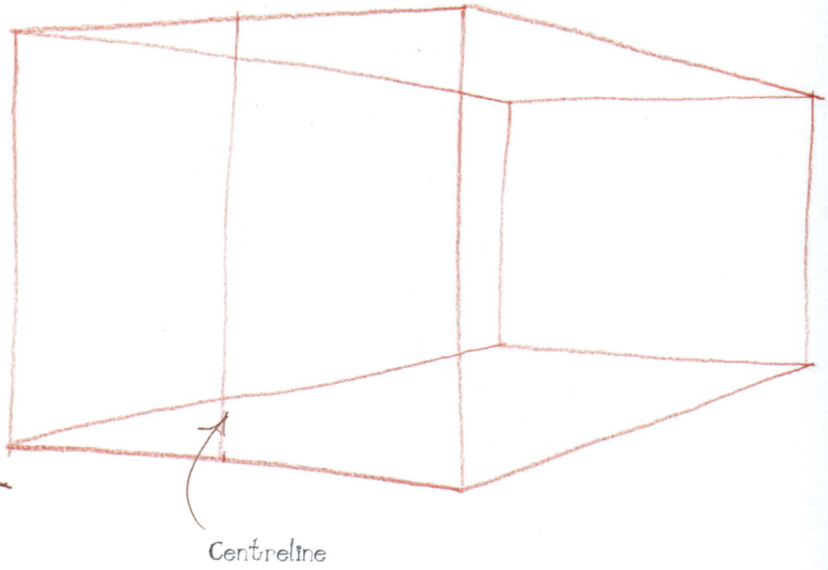

Now draw the main body of the taxi. Mark the windscreen and position of the wheels.

Don't forget to add the distinctive taxi sign on the roof.

Mark lines on the taxi for the doors and windows.

The car's wheel arch follows the direction of the perspective box. Indicate wheel rims with smaller ellipses.

Add shading to the taxi. Leave some parts white as highlights.

The position of the wipers can indicate the weather.

Add shading underneath the taxi.

Lighthouses and towers

Drawing tall objects from low or high angles is an effective way in which perspective can lend a sense of scale and visual impact to your subject.

Lighthouse at Beachy Head near Eastbourne, Sussex.

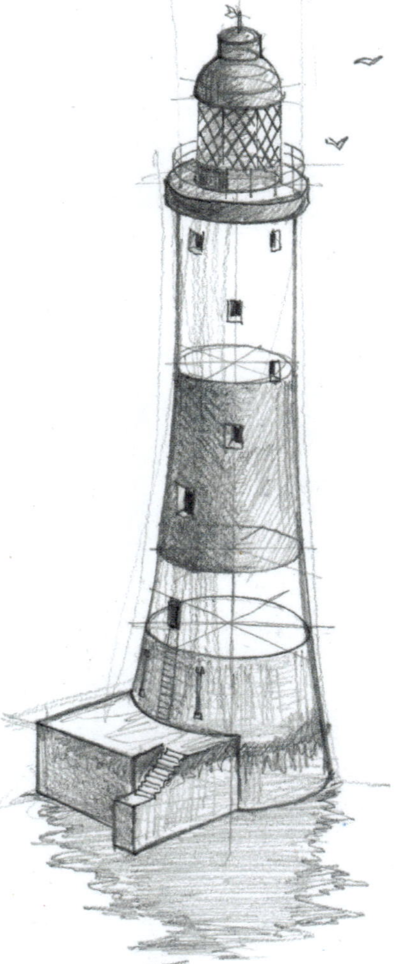

Use construction lines to give your drawings solidity and accuracy.

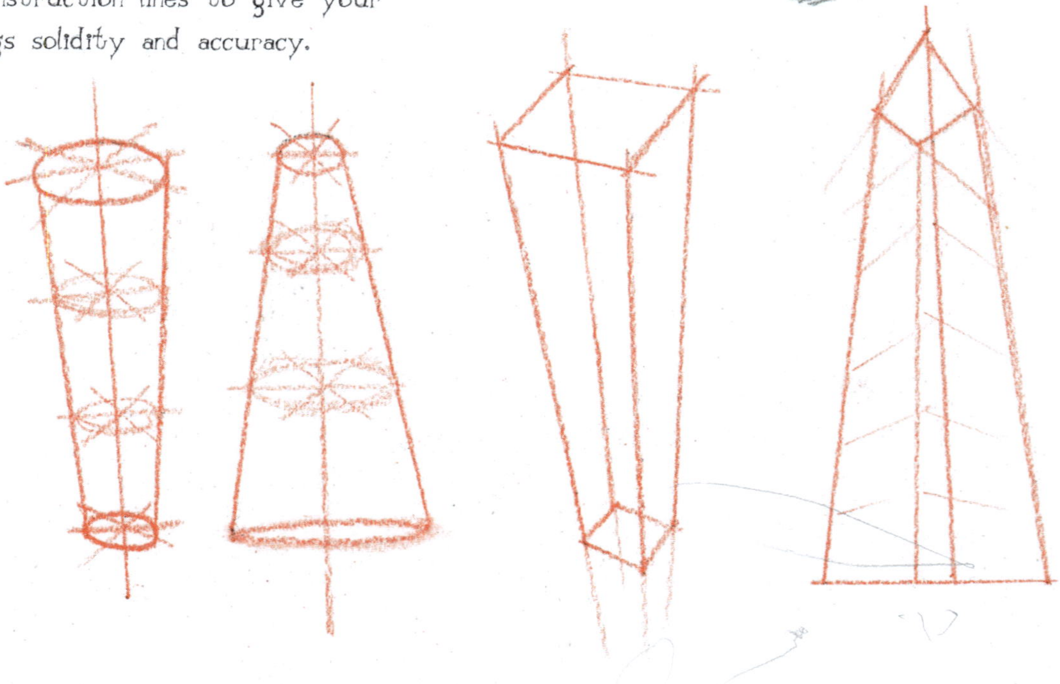

St Mark's Square, Venice

This low-angle view makes the tower seem spectacularly tall and imposing.

Giotto's Bell Tower, Florence

This high-angle bird's eye view of the tower gives a real sense of its scale and height in relation to the surrounding cityscape.

Castles

Castles and palaces can be found in all different, fantastic shapes across the world, from Europe to India and the Middle East. The often irregular, ornate nature of their designs is ideal for 3D drawing.

Start by drawing a box using perspective lines.

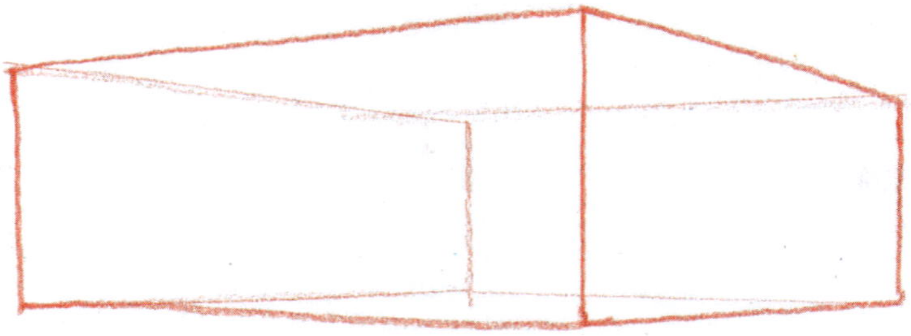

Carefully plot out vanishing points to the left and right.

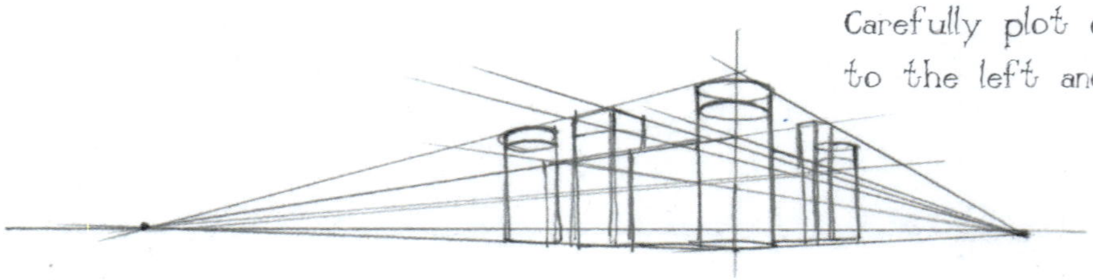

Start to draw in the towers. Pay close attention to each V.P.

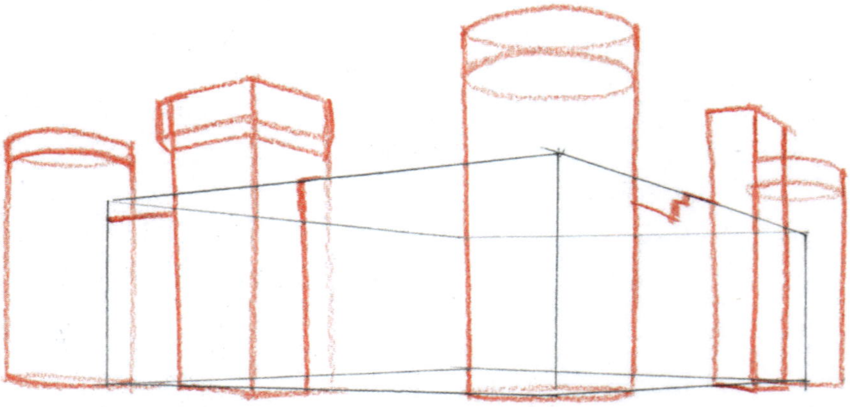

Now add in further details like the windows, crenellations and any decorative features. Indicate the treeline beyond the castle.

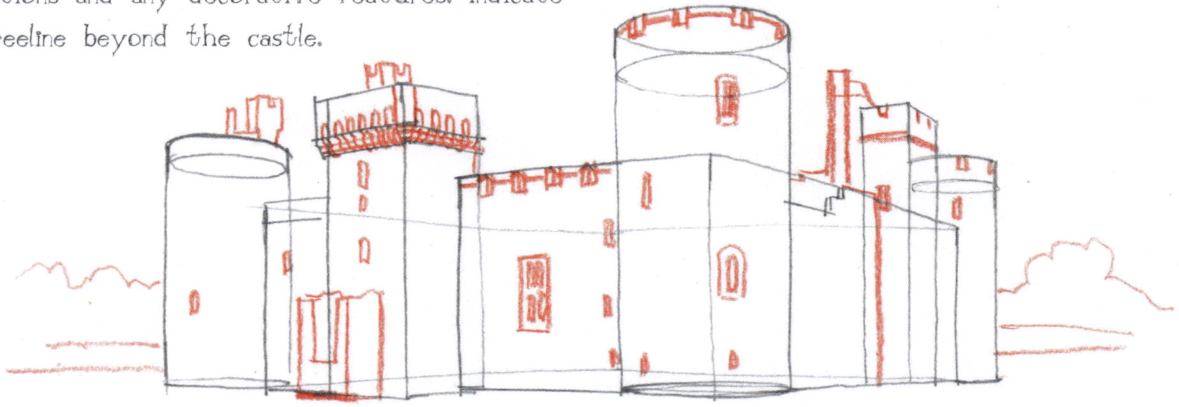

Decide on your light source and then add shading to areas where light would not reach. Finish off the background details and add the castle's reflection in the surrounding moat.

Bodiam Castle in East Sussex

Depth and perspective

To make your drawings feel three-dimensional, it is important to give a sense of depth – of objects in both the foreground and the background of the picture.

Here the zig-zagging road guides the viewer's eye towards the farthest point.

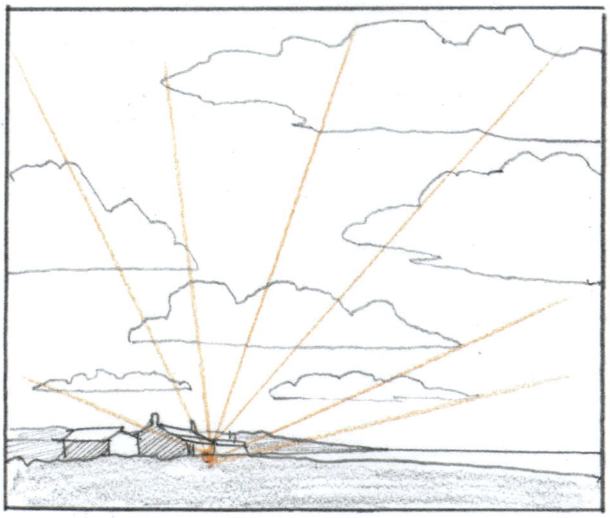

The rocks at the bottom of the lefthand picture, and the clouds at the top of the righthand picture, help to create a sense of depth and immersive three-dimensionality.

Here the road rolling over the hills emphasises the depth of the picture.

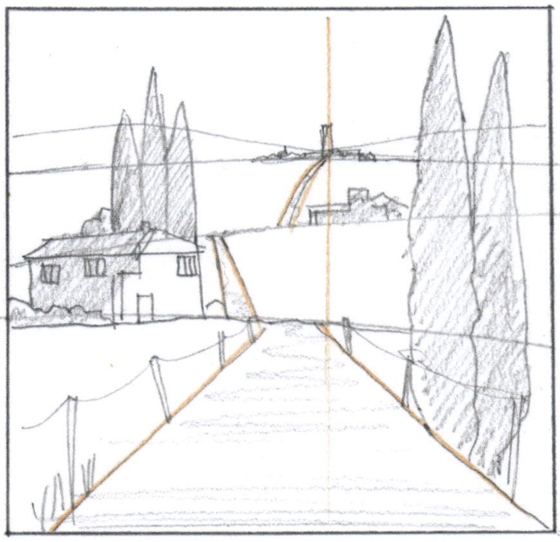

It can be useful to employ grids to map out towns and cities when drawing them, as their layouts can be complex.

Always keep the vanishing point in mind. This image has one V.P. just to the left of the centre of the frame.

View from a window

Drawing pictures of views and landscapes through windows is a visually interesting way of emphasising perspective and the three-dimensional quality of what is being depicted.

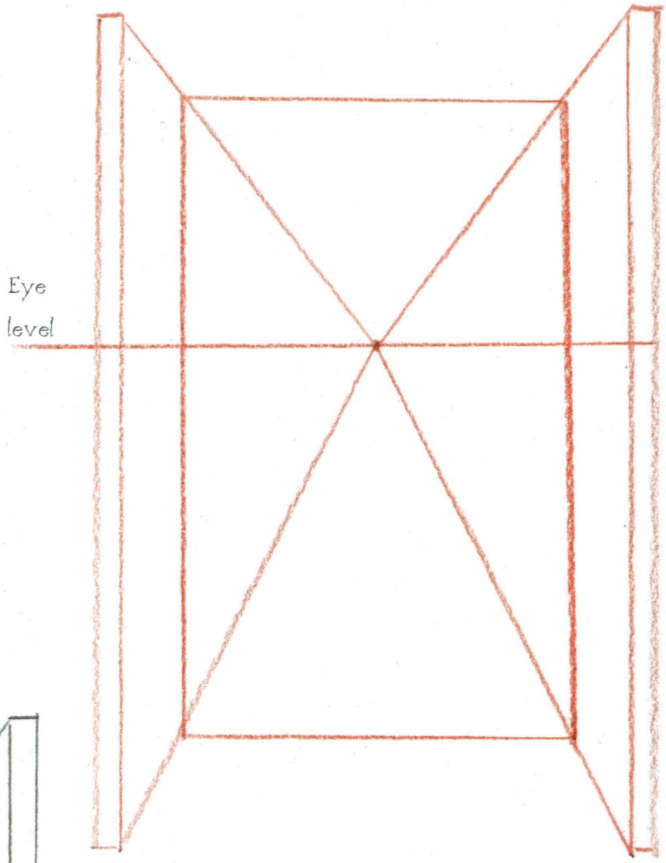

Begin by drawing the window frame and the construction lines converging on a single vanishing point.

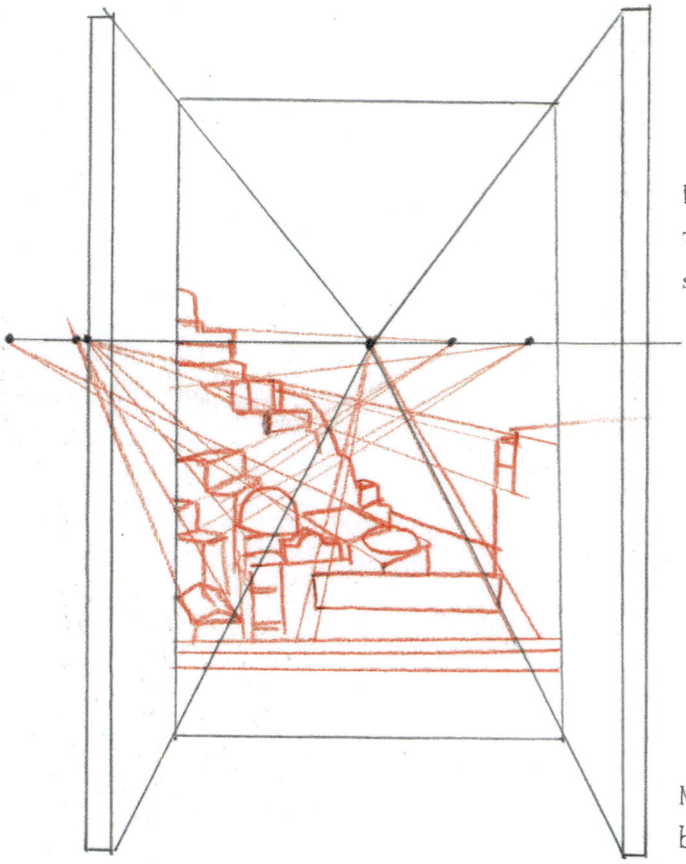

Now start drawing in the town below, stretching away to the left of the frame.

Next, sketch in the shoreline beyond the town and add further details to the outlines of the houses.

The window slats should also converge towards the single vanishing point.

Add shading to the landscape and draw in the balcony outside the window to emphasise the feeling of depth.

Leading the eye

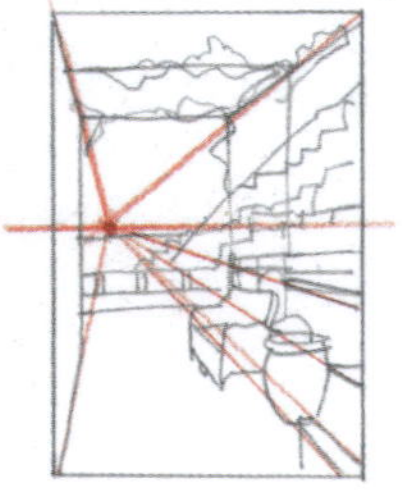

There are various tricks and techniques of composition that can be used to lead a viewer's eye through a picture and strengthen the illusion of it being three-dimensional.

Durdle Door in Dorset

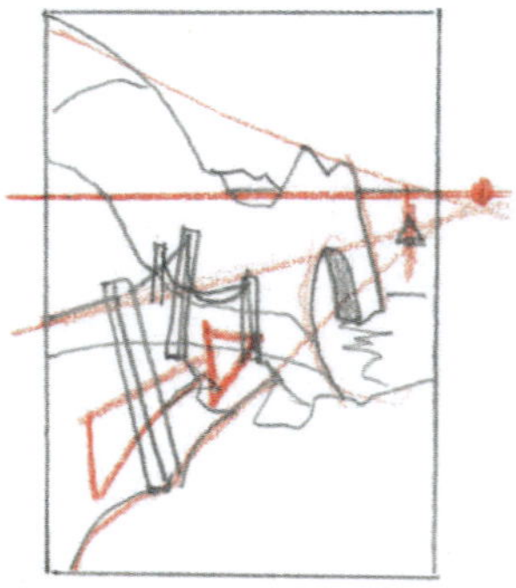

The wooden posts and rocky outcrop lead your eye along a diagonal path ending at the boat.

Italian street scene

The tall building and the shadow cast from the plant pot draw the eye to the very top and bottom of the picture, emphasising the spatial element of the drawing.

Shading is used to lead the eye and create depth here. The lightness of the background landscape, stretching to the vanishing point, guides the eye away from the shadowed foreground.

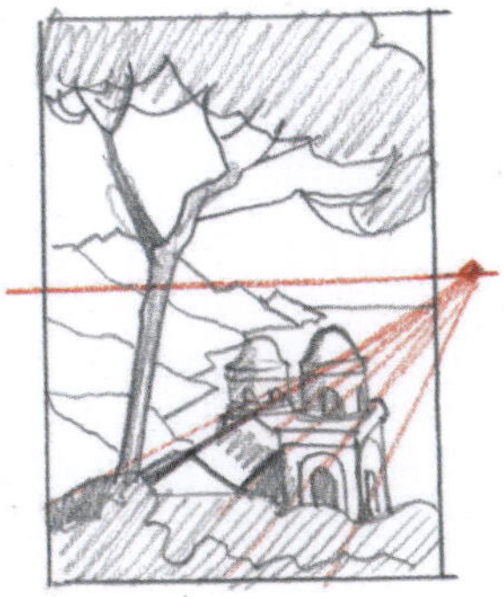

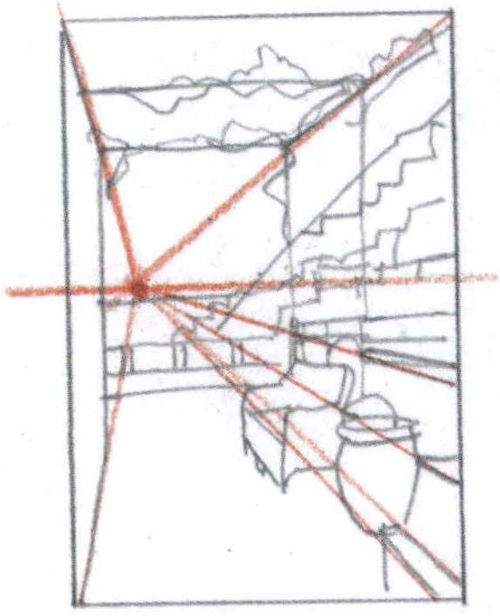

The positioning of the furniture on the patio leads the eye towards the vanishing point out at sea.

How to turn 2D into 3D

It is possible to quickly make a drawing that has the illusion of being three-dimensional simply by including one or a few 3D objects within it and leaving the rest flat.

Begin by drawing in the front of the castle in 2D.

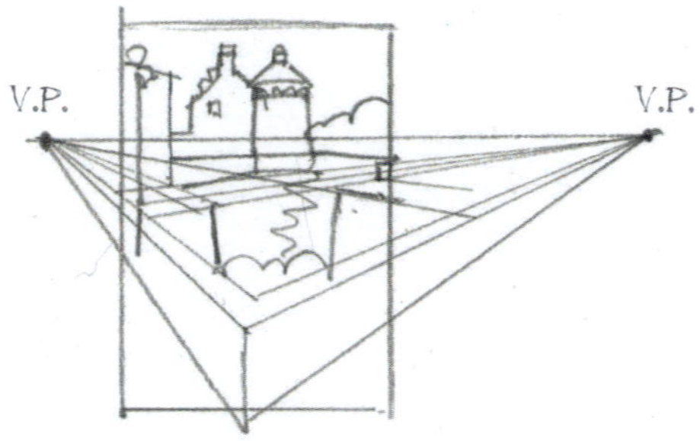

Now add the wall in the foreground, stretching away towards the two vanishing points on the left and right of the frame.

Draw in the other main elements of the picture, such as the bricks, water, windows and bushes

Scotney Castle in Kent

Finally, add the reflection of the castle in the water and shade in the picture.

Bowl of fruit

A bowl of fruit is a classic still-life composition. Many famous artists have drawn still lifes of fruit. It is worth researching other artists for inspiration!

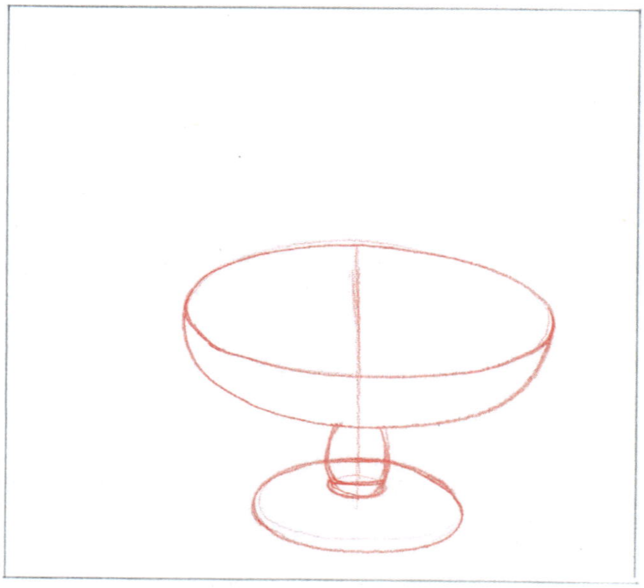

Start by sketching out the shape of the bowl as a wire-frame outline.

Sketch in the shape of the overlapping fruit. Keep these construction lines faint so they can be easily erased.

Using a mirror

Try looking at your drawing in a mirror. Seeing it in reverse can help you spot mistakes.

Indicate the folds of the drapery. Add more form and detail to the fruit shapes.

Add shading to the individual fruit and the various parts of the bowl. This will give your finished drawing a three-dimensional effect.

Glossary

Composition The arrangement of the parts of a picture on the drawing paper.

Construction lines Guidelines used in the early stages of a drawing; they may be erased later.

Cross-hatching An area of crisscross lines used to create a dark tone.

Light source The direction from which the light seems to come in a drawing.

Perspective A method of drawing in which near objects are shown larger than faraway objects to give an impression of depth.

Tone (or shading) The use of light and dark areas in a drawing to give a three-dimensional effect.

Vanishing point The place in a perspective drawing where lines that are really parallel appear to meet.

Index